- THE LEGEND OF -
BAEOH

How Baeoh Got His Stripes

L E A D E R S H I P

Written by Lucas Taekwon Lee

Illustrations by Max Forward

Design & Layout by LukaszDesign.com

Robert D. Reed Publishers
P.O. Box 1992 • Bandon, OR 97411
Phone: 541-347-9882; Fax: -9883
E-mail: 4bobreed@msn.com
Website: www.rdrpublishers.com

ISBN: 978-1-931741-88-0
Printed in China.

For generations, there was a peace between the tigers and the jackals in Songahm Jungle.

The law of the jungle said the tigers must live in the highlands, and the jackals must live in the lowlands.

The leadership and hierarchy of tigers was dictated by the number of stripes on their coat.

The 3-Stripe Tigers were on the top of the chain and ruled the jungle for generations. After them were the 2-Stripe Tigers, then the 1-Stripe Tigers.

The lowest class were the tigers without any stripes. They lived in the middle lands, just above the jackals.

Baeoh was born with no stripes.

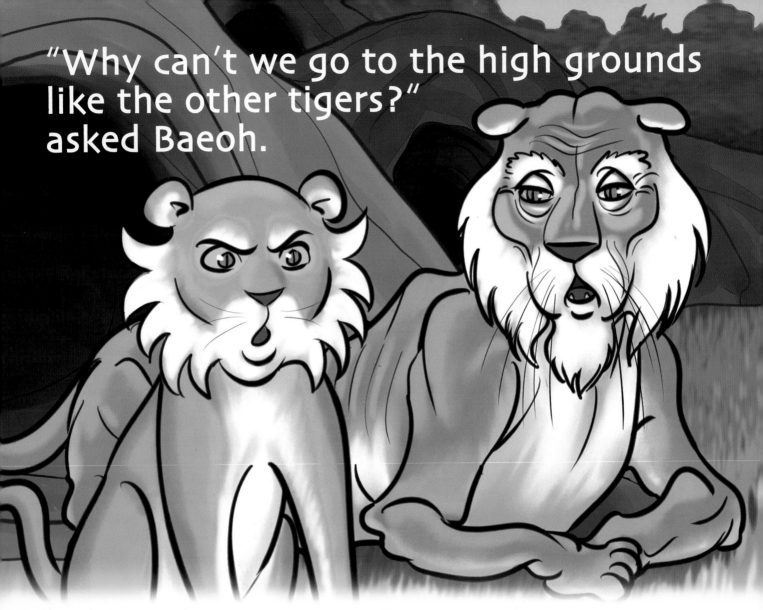

"Why can't we go to the high grounds like the other tigers?" asked Baeoh.

"This is where we belong," said his Uncle Hiyun.

"But what makes the 3-Stripe Tigers better than us?" asked Baeoh. "Destiny," answered his uncle. "We are destined to serve the 3-Stripe Tigers."

The days went on and Baeoh's patience was tested.

One day he confessed his frustration to his mother, "I respect the law, but I do not accept that it is our destiny to be peasants."

His mother then told him a story that most tigers had long forgotten.

"Thousands of years ago when tigers and jackals were at war, there was a tiger who had no stripes but overcame his hardships with confidence, courage, and leadership. His bravery and skills were greater even than the 3-Stripe Tigers.

"One day he leaped in the air to defend some of his fellow tigers and a miraculous thing happened... he began to fly!

"The battle stopped... and all the tigers and jackals froze in disbelief.

"From then on, the Flying Tiger became a leader in the jungle and brought peace to the land!"

"How did the tiger fly?" asked Baeoh. "He didn't even have any stripes!" "He had the courage to believe he could achieve more than society told him," his mother replied.

Inspired by the story of the Flying Tiger, Baeoh was now even more determined to change his destiny.

"I want to achieve great things also, but I cannot do so if I stay here."

Baeoh's mother worried for her son, but she knew his adventurous spirit would not allow him to stay. So Baeoh decided to leave the safety of his tribe in search of truth.

Days had passed as Baeoh explored the jungle.

After many weeks he no longer knew how to get home. This was a very strange land for the young tiger.

All of a sudden, a pack of jackals surrounded Baeoh! With their teeth snarling, they drew closer and attacked!

But just as he thought the end was coming... the snarling turned into whimpering.

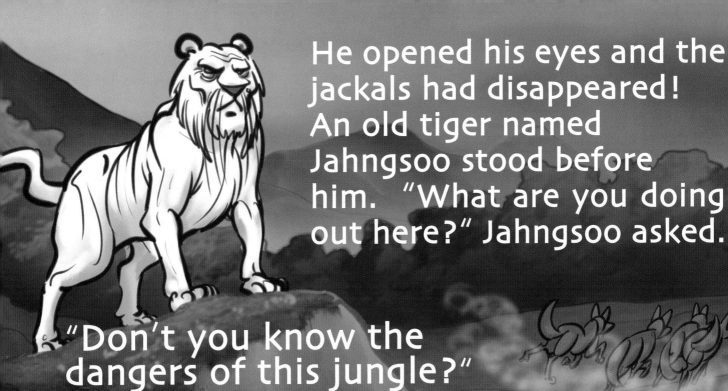

He opened his eyes and the jackals had disappeared! An old tiger named Jahngsoo stood before him. "What are you doing out here?" Jahngsoo asked.

"Don't you know the dangers of this jungle?"

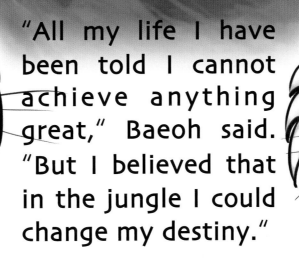

"All my life I have been told I cannot achieve anything great," Baeoh said. "But I believed that in the jungle I could change my destiny."

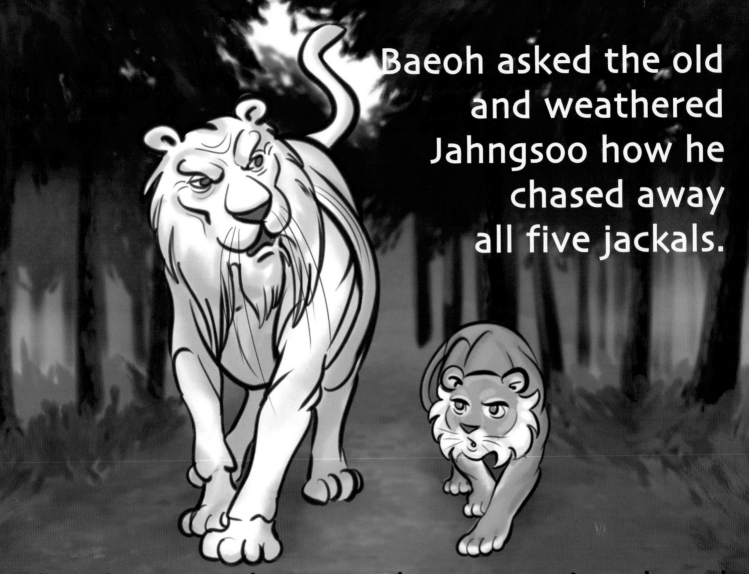

Baeoh asked the old and weathered Jahngsoo how he chased away all five jackals.

"Little Tiger, do not make assumptions based on physical appearance," Jahngsoo said.

"You have much to learn!" From then on, Baeoh followed Jahngsoo and began to learn new lessons in his life.

With perseverance, Baeoh endured the training that pushed his body to the limit. Days turned into weeks as Jahngsoo challenged Baeoh to train harder.

Weeks turned into months as Baeoh grew into a strong tiger.

Then, after a long day of grueling exercises they stood in front of a mighty river. Jahngsoo instructed Baeoh to jump across the entire river in one leap.

"The river is at least twenty times the length of my body!" worried Baeoh. "If I fall, the strength of the river might sweep me away!"
"You must try your best," said Jahngsoo.

With doubt, Baeoh jumped as far as he could, but he fell before even making it half way across.

Panicked, he swam back to the shore coughing and sputtering.

"It's no use," Baeoh said. "I do not have enough strength to cross this river."

"That is because you do not believe," Jahngsoo said. "How do you expect to do it without any confidence?"

Baeoh shook off the water from his coat. Looking at the river with determination, he stepped back and jumped with all his might!

This time, he made it half way across the river, but he still fell into the water. The current was very strong and he needed to be saved from the river by Jahngsoo.

"We both know I am not strong enough," said Baeoh. "After all, I am a lowly peasant tiger. Besides, how will jumping over the river help me become a leader?"

"Little Tiger, in this jungle you will be tested by things much more dangerous than a river," answered Jahngsoo. "It is now time to allow your courage to find your nobility!"

Baeoh was angry and frustrated but even more determined. He hadn't come so far to quit now.

He had to believe he could achieve what he thought was impossible.

He mustered all the strength he had left and ran as fast as he could toward the riverbank.

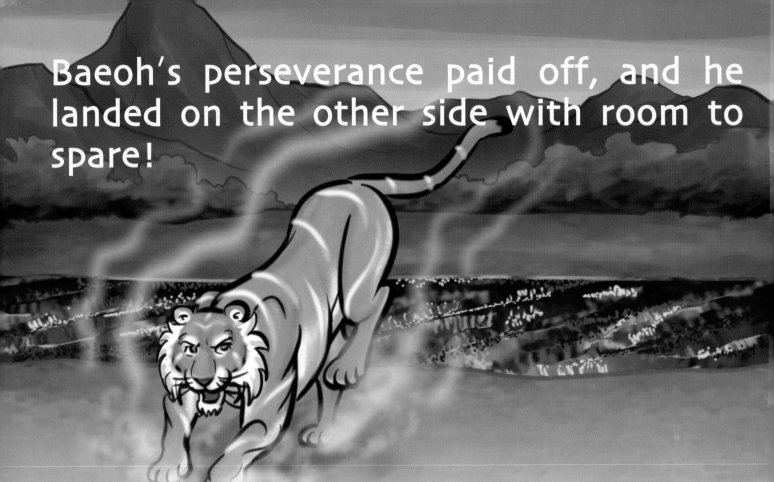

Baeoh's perseverance paid off, and he landed on the other side with room to spare!

With excitement, he exclaimed, "I did it! I did it!"

All of a sudden, a stripe magically appeared on Baeoh's coat!

He looked down at his fur and boasted, **"I have a stripe! Look at me!"**

Suddenly Jahngsoo appeared next to him and said, "Baeoh, you must remain confident, yet also humble."

"But how did I get this stripe on my coat?" asked Baeoh. "All my life, I have been powerless and without a stripe. Now, I have enough strength to leap a river and I have a stripe!"

Jahngsoo reminded him, "It is not how powerful you are that is important. It is how you choose to apply your power that truly makes you great."

They then heard snarling sounds from the other side of the river. A very weak and injured tiger was trying to fend off four jackals!

"Remember, your strength has been tested," Jahngsoo said. "Now you must choose how to use it."

A jackal pounced on top of the Weak Tiger and drew his deadly teeth close. Without time to think, Baeoh leaped across the river, this time with ease.

The jackals quickly turned their fighting snarls toward Baeoh.

In one pounce Baeoh had all four jackals pinned. "You should not pick on the weak because you never know who stands behind him!" roared Baeoh.

As he drew his jaws closer he heard the wise voice of Jahngsoo... "Power should never be used to harm those weaker than you."

Baeoh then set the jackals free, and they quickly disappeared, whimpering into the jungle. Weak Tiger stood up and bowed his head to Baeoh and said, "Thank you! I thought my life was doomed, but I have been saved by a 2-Stripe Tiger!"

Baeoh looked down and to his surprise, he did not see just one stripe anymore, but two!

Weak Tiger began to explain to Baeoh about the jackals' plan to take over the tiger tribes, "You must return to the tribes."

"The jackals have found a way to defeat the tigers! It will be the end of our way of life as we know it."

The two tigers began their trek back to the tiger tribes. Jahngsoo had disappeared, but Baoeh knew he must believe in what he had learned in order to save his village.

The lessons of confidence, courage, and perseverance were all making sense.

Days had passed and the two tigers finally arrived at the tribes.

Every tiger was astonished upon seeing Baeoh, especially his proud mother. She said tearfully, "Son, I cannot believe you are standing in front of me. How did you get these stripes on your coat?"

Baeoh replied, "Mother, thank you for helping me see that I can achieve so much in my life.
I have learned that with courage I can accomplish things I did not think were possible."

Weak Tiger suddenly declared with urgency, "I have been trying to tell this to the elders: The jackals' revolt is coming!

"The 3-Stripe Tigers are away at the top of the hill and do not care about us! Baeoh must save the tribes!"

At that moment, appearing from the bushes, the jackals began closing in on the tigers. The jackals' revolt had begun!

The leader of the jackals came forward and said, "Tigers, for generations you have repressed us. We have always lived in your shadow. From this day on, you must live under our laws!"

All the tigers bowed down to the Jackal Leader except Baeoh, who remained confident and stood tall.

Seeing this, the Jackal Leader snarled, "Foolish tiger, do you wish to be the sacrifice for your tribes?"

Baeoh replied calmly, "The greatest power I have is not the strength to attack. It is the power to choose right from wrong and the choice to teach others the same."

With this act of nobility and leadership, a third stripe appeared on Baeoh's coat, now making him a 3-Stripe Tiger!

Seeing this, the other tigers became emboldened and declared, "Baeoh has three stripes! We can now defeat the jackals once and for all and rule the jungle forever!"

But to everyone's surprise, Baeoh stood between the tigers and the jackals and said, "We will not attack the jackals just to show that we are more powerful than they are."

"The greatest leadership is to use our strength to help those weaker than ourselves. We must learn to live with the jackals in harmony. If we share our leadership with them, their strength will help us just as our strength will help them.

Our destiny is not bound by birth. It is only bound by honor, courage, respect, nobility, and leadership."

From that day forward, the tigers and jackals of Songahm Jungle lived in peace and unity.

Baeoh's destiny was never written for him. He chose to become a leader in his jungle through nobility.

If your life is a book, only yesterday and the days before are written; your future is for you to write.

What is in your book?

What is your destiny?

MARTIAL ARTS

Only you can write the pages of your life.

What are your goals?

In 1 month, I will:

In 1 year, I will:

In 5 years, I will:

AS A TINY TIGER, YOU CAN EARN YOUR STRIPES JUST LIKE BAEOH!

When you achieve your stripes, color in Baeoh's stripes too!

Ask your instructor or parent for permission.

Like Baeoh, I have earned:

__ 1 stripe   date:_____

__ 2 stripes   date:_____

__ 3 stripes   date:_____